W9-BUS-287

DATE DUE _____

WITHDRAWN FROM
COLLECTION

Come On, Rain!

by **Karen Hesse**

pictures by **Jon J Muth**

Scholastic Press   New York

To my mother . . . in celebration of all our summers

—K. H.

For Adelaine and Nikolai

—J. M.

"Come on, rain!" I say,

squinting into the endless heat.

Mamma lifts a listless vine and sighs.
"Three weeks and not a drop,"
she says, sagging over her parched plants.

The sound of a heavy truck rumbles past.

Uneasy, Mamma looks over to me. "Is that thunder, Tessie?" she asks.

Mamma hates thunder. I climb up the steps for a better look.

"It's just a truck, Mamma," I say.

I am sizzling like a hot potato.

I ask Mamma, "May I put on my bathing suit?"

"Absolutely not," Mamma says, frowning under her straw hat.

"You'll burn all day out in this sun."

Up and down the block,

cats pant,

heat wavers off tar patches in the broiling alleyway.

Miz Grace and Miz Vera bend, tending beds of drooping lupines.

Not a sign of my friends Liz or Rosemary,

not a peep from my pal Jackie-Joyce.

I stare out over rooftops,

past chimneys, into the way off distance.

And that's when I see it coming,

clouds rolling in,

gray clouds, bunched and bulging under a purple sky.

A creeper of hope circles 'round my bones.

"Come on, rain!" I whisper.

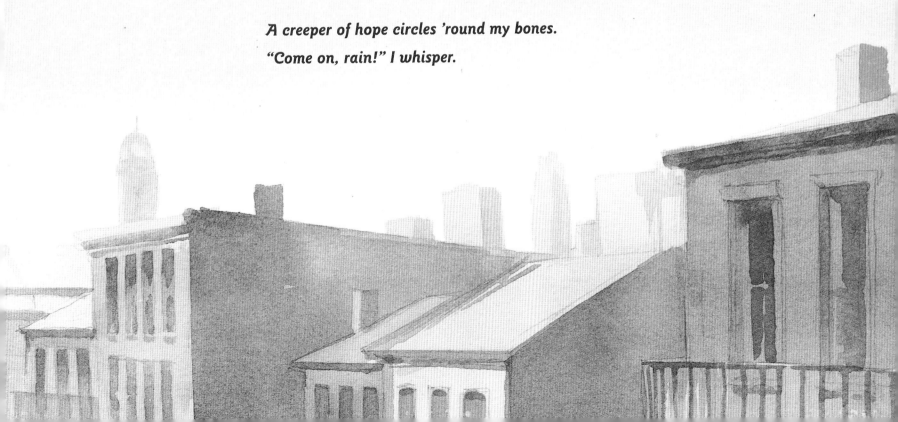

Quietly,

while Mamma weeds,

I cross the crackling-dry path past Miz Glick's window . . .

. . . *glancing inside as I hurry by.*
Miz Glick's needle sticks on her phonograph,
playing the same notes over and over
in the dim, stuffy cave of her room.

The smell of hot tar and garbage bullies the air
as I climb the steps to Jackie-Joyce's porch.
"Jackie-Joyce?" I breathe, pressing my nose against her screen.

Jackie-Joyce comes to the door.
Her long legs, like two brown string beans,
sprout from her shorts.
"It's going to rain," I whisper.
"Put on your suit and come straight over."

Slick with sweat,
I run back home and slip up the steps past Mamma.
She is nearly senseless in the sizzling heat,
kneeling over the hot rump of a melon.

In the kitchen, I pour iced tea to the top
of a tall glass.
I aim a spoonful of sugar into my mouth,
then a second into the drink.

"Got you some tea, Mamma," I say,
pulling her inside the house.

Mamma sinks onto a kitchen chair
and sweeps off her hat.
Sweat trickles down her neck
and wets the front of her dress
and under her arms.
Mamma presses the ice-chilled glass against her skin.
"Aren't you something, Tessie," she says.
I nod, smartly.
"Rain's coming, Mamma," I say.

Mamma turns to the window and sniffs.
"It's about time," she murmurs.

Jackie-Joyce, in her bathing suit,
knocks at the door, and I let her in.

"Jackie-Joyce has her suit on, Mamma," I say.
"May I wear mine, too?"

I hold my breath,
waiting.
A breeze blows the thin curtains into the kitchen,
then sucks them back against the screen again.

"Is there thunder?" Mamma asks.
        "No thunder," I say.
"Is there lightning?" Mamma asks.
        "No lightning," Jackie-Joyce says.
"You stay where I can find you," Mamma says.
        "We will," I say.
"Go on then," Mamma says,
lifting the glass to her lips to take a sip.

"Come on, rain!" I cheer,
peeling out of my clothes and into my suit,
while Jackie-Joyce runs to get
Liz and Rosemary.

We meet in the alleyway.

All the insects have gone still.

Trees sway under a swollen sky,

the wind grows bold and bolder,

. . . and just like that,

rain comes.

The first drops plop down big,

making dust dance all around us.

Then a deeper gray descends
and the air cools and the clouds burst,

and suddenly
rain is everywhere.

"Come on, rain!" we shout.

It streams through our hair and down our backs.
It freckles our feet, glazes our toes.
We turn in circles,
glistening in our rain skin.
Our mouths wide,
we gulp down rain.

Jackie-Joyce chases Rosemary

who chases Liz

who chases me.

Wet slicking our arms and legs, we splash up the block,

squealing and whooping in the streaming rain.

We make such a racket,
Miz Glick rushes out on her porch.
Miz Grace and Miz Vera come next,
and then comes Mamma.
They run from their kitchens and skid to a stop.

Leaning over their rails, they turn to each other.
A smile spreads from porch to porch.
And with a wordless nod . . .

. . . *first one, then all* . . .

. . . *fling off their shoes,*
skim off their hose,
tossing streamers of stockings over their shoulders.
Our barelegged mammas dance down the steps
and join us in the fresh, clean rain . . .

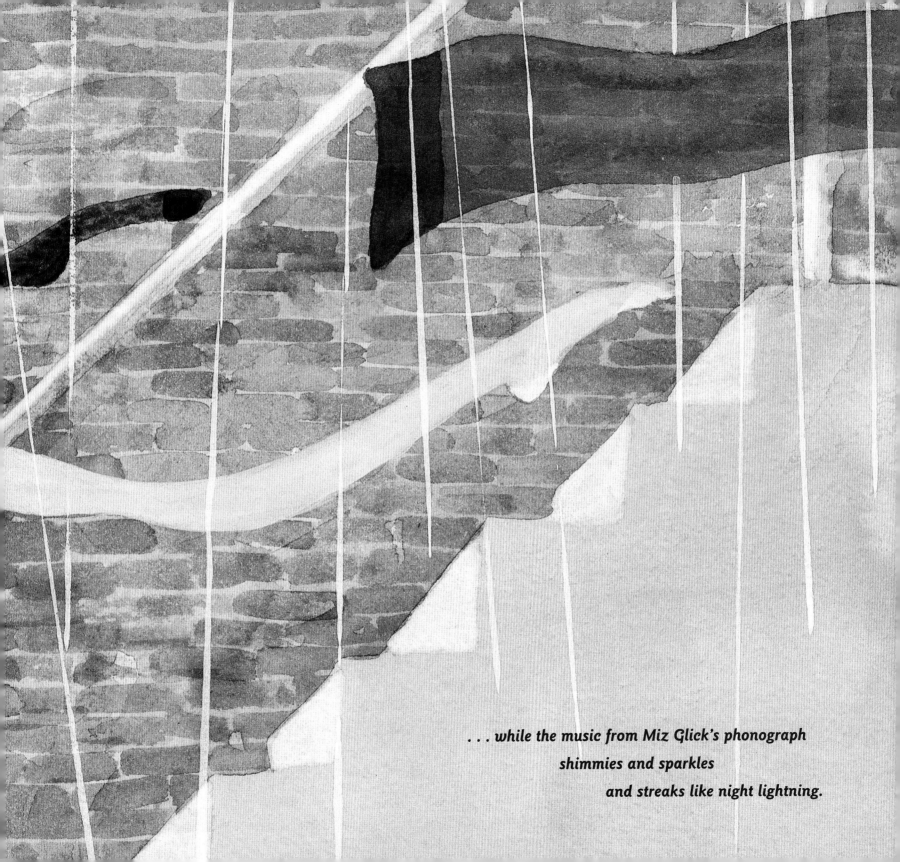

. . . while the music from Miz Glick's phonograph
shimmies and sparkles
and streaks like night lightning.

Jackie-Joyce, Liz, Rosemary and I,
we grab the hands of our mammas.
We twirl and sway them,
tromping through puddles,
romping and reeling in the moisty green air.

We swing our wet and wild-haired mammas 'til we're all laughing
under trinkets of silver rain.

I hug Mamma hard,
and she hugs me back.
The rain has made us new.

As the clouds move off,
I trace the drips on Mamma's face.
Everywhere, everyone, everything
is misty limbs, springing back to life.

"We sure did get a soaking, Mamma," I say,

and we head home

purely soothed,

fresh as dew,

turning toward the first sweet rays of the sun.

A shower of thanks

to Mark Breen of the Fairbanks Museum,

to Lois, Cookie, Bonnie, and Janet,

Miz Dot, Miz Chippy, Mom, and Miz Frances,

to Eileen, Bob, Liza, and Randy,

to Kate and Rachel,

  and Dianne Hess

Text copyright © 1999 by Karen Hesse

Illustrations copyright © 1999 by Jon J Muth

All rights reserved. Published by Scholastic Press, a division of Scholastic Inc.,

Publishers since 1920. SCHOLASTIC and SCHOLASTIC PRESS and associated logos are trademarks

and/or registered trademarks of Scholastic Inc.

Library of Congress Cataloging-in-Publication Data

Hesse, Karen.

Come on, rain! / by Karen Hesse ; illustrated by Jon J Muth.   p.   cm.

Summary: A young girl eagerly awaits a coming rainstorm to bring relief from the oppressive

summer heat.   ISBN 0-590-33125-6

[1. Rain and rainfall — Fiction. 2. Summer — Fiction. 3. Mothers and daughters — Fiction.]

I. Muth, Jon J, ill. II. Title.   PZ7.H4364Rai 1999   98-11575   CIP   AC

Printed in the U.S.A   36

10 9 8 7 6 5 4 3 2 1   02 01 0/0 9/9

First edition, March 1999

Book design by David Saylor

The text type was set in 13-point Goudy Sans Bold Italic.

The illustrations in this book were rendered in watercolor.